Scion™

Conflict of Conscience

D1558295

Chapter 1

1.5

2

3

4

5

6

7

CREATORS

Ron Marz
Writer

Jim Cheung
Penciler

Don Hillsman II
Inker

Caesar Rodriguez
Colorist

Dave Lanphear
Letterer

SCION #7

Rick Leonardi
Penciler

Karl Kesel
Inker

Paul Mounts
Colorist

CROSSGEN CHRONICLES #1

Ron Marz with Barbara Kesel
Writers

Claudio Castellini
Penciler

Caesar Rodriguez with Andrew Crossley
CG Inkers

Michael Atiyeh
Colorist

The CrossGen Universe created by Mark Alessi & Gina M. Villa

TRADE PAPERBACK

Cover Illustrated by Adam Hughes

DESIGN

Pam Davies
Dave Lanphear
Brandon Peterson
Sylvia Bretz
Troy Peteri

EDITORIAL

Tony Panaccio
Ian M. Feller
Barbara Kesel
Mark Waid
Ron Marz
Bart Sears
Gina M. Villa

FOREWORD

The hardest thing you'll ever do is the right thing.

And it's not like there is a dearth of choices for us in this life. We are faced with choices every day that tease us and vex us. Go to work or call in sick, the burger or the veggie platter, regular unleaded or premium. All these little choices pile up every day, and some are pretty clear. If you're watching your weight, you don't have to be Dr. Stephen Hawking to do the math between choosing the salad or the Big Mac.

But it's not just the little ones, all cumulatively stacked in a heap, that get to us. When they're combined with the big ones – where to work, where to live, who to marry – that's where we can tend to get confused.

Then why is doing the right thing so hard for so many of us? In literature, how is it that we can segregate the villains from the heroes based on these choices? Because it's the struggle, not the victory, that makes the hero.

However, in the last few decades of comics, I discovered a trend that disturbed me: heroes were being made from characters whose victories came at any price. These heroes were willing to kill without conscience, able to ignore suffering if it wasn't directly related to their cause. These were heroes who didn't struggle to win but, rather, frequently took the easy route to victory.

CrossGen was founded, in part, as a response to this trend. As one of our primary missions, we wanted to find a way to tell stories about three simple principles: Might for right, coming of age, and coming to responsibility. These were the themes that have been prevalent for several thousand years of heroic fiction, themes common when I was reading comics as a kid. Those were the comics that inspired me as an adult to collect comics and comic book art. My goal was to make this type of comic book popular again, to demonstrate that you didn't have to show gratuitous violence or blatant sexuality – without any hint of a moral code – in order to make good comics. Instead, all you needed was a good story developed with an understanding of how intelligent and sophisticated today's readers are, painstakingly executed artwork, and a staff of creators willing to roll the dice on a dream.

Scion is one of the cornerstones of how

that dream is fast becoming reality. The story of the young Heron prince Ethan, *Scion* begins as a crisis of conscience that drives the prince to reconsider all his preconceived notions of life. To royalty, there is a natural, ordained order to things. Our pursuit was to see what happens when something disturbs that natural order and to challenge Ethan to take on that journey.

As you read, you'll see that many of the choices laid down before Ethan are not easy ones. Most of the time, he's given choices that are both right and wrong at the same time. Whenever Ethan finds himself at a fork in the road where taking either path will be difficult and not likely very rewarding, it's not always easy to predict where he will go. Not only does that make for the creation of a potentially epic heroic character, but it also makes for a good, solid read.

It's not difficult to figure out why we decided to include a medieval tale of knights and battles in the CrossGen Universe – especially if you look at my bookshelf and see the collected editions of Hal Foster's classic newspaper comic strip, *Prince Valiant*. When laying down the skeleton for our first four comic book titles – which later were named *Mystic, Sigil, Scion* and *Meridian* – we knew that sword-and-sorcery fantasy was one of the great non-superhero genres in the history of comics. But we wanted to include a twist, so we eliminated the sorcery aspect and, in its place, inserted science fiction. We envisioned a world in which technology was intermingled with the conventions of medieval literature, creating a fresh viewpoint and potential for far more original stories than have been attempted in this medium for some time.

With this mission, this anti-formula and this inspiration, we turned *Scion* over to Ron Marz, Jim Cheung, Don Hillsman II, and Caesar Rodriguez to create a new world for us and for you. We've populated this world with knights, tournaments, damsels (but not necessarily in distress), bounty hunters, flying dragons with on-board computers, evil warmongers, and the supernatural presence of the Sigil, CrossGen's talisman of power. There is action, adventure, intrigue, deception and one of the most amazingly depicted medieval combat scenes of any modern comic book ever published.

But at the center of all of this is a young man who is about to learn just how hard it really is to do the right thing. ☯

Mark Alessi

This place grows colder, my friend. Its energy wanes. I am seeking a solution, and eagerly welcome your thoughts.

It is not like you to be so troubled.

So long ago, when it was all set in motion, it was so... fascinating in its complexity. It surprised even me. Now things are static, worlds grow cold, and what were once glorious fields of battle lay still and barren.

The problem is not simply lazy warriors. The vital energies on which we all depend are fading away... it shouldn't happen like this... yet it is! It is dying, and the first do nothing to prevent it!

Because the First don't understand. They have no idea of the connection between their actions and the Whole.

Yes. They need...motivation. They must be forced to reignite the cycle...

Yet...they know nothing of my existence. To do so would *change* them...

Chapter

1

Why look only to the First?

Ah... this was my first world.

Time and evolution have changed it from the simple world it was. But look at how it has grown!

New races of man have even been created, although I see that they are treated as less than men.

Yet we've seen little battle of late. Their mock combat needs to be hammered into the steel of true war. Their old hatreds need to burn again.

SIMPLE ENOUGH, IF YOU FOLLOW *YOUR* PLAN...

WHAT WILL I TELL THEM, THESE... *SIGIL-BEARERS?*

GIVE THEM NO WARNING, NO DIRECTION; LET THEIR ACTIONS DICTATE THE FLARE OF THE SIGIL.

THIS WILL REENERGIZE YOUR WARRIORS. BRING THEM BACK TO THEIR PURPOSE. HAVE THEM FIGHT OFF THE CHILL OF THEIR CURRENT ENNUI.

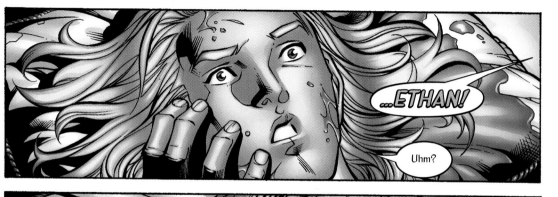

ETHAN, I'M SORRY. I COULDN'T *STOP* THEM.

IT'S ALL RIGHT, ONLY A LITTLE WATER.

MY BROTHERS WERE JUST HAVING SOME FUN.

DEET

STILL, THEY DIDN'T *NEED* TO.

SOMETIMES THEY DON'T THINK ABOUT THE THINGS THEY DO.

FSSSSSSSZZ

MY BEST WISHES ON YOUR BIRTHDAY, OF COURSE. TWENTY-ONE ALREADY. IT HARDLY SEEMS THE YEARS COULD'VE PASSED SO QUICKLY.

YOUR BLUE TUNIC?

THAT'S FINE. THANKS.

IT'S UNDERSTANDABLE TO BE NERVOUS. YOUR FIRST COMBAT, AND IN FRONT OF SO MANY

YOUR *MOTHER'S* QUITE WORRIED, YOU KNOW.

15

OF COURSE SHE'S WORRIED. SHE'S MY MOTHER, IT'S WHAT SHE DOES.

SHE HAS GOOD REASON.

THERE'S SOMETHING YOU NEED TO KNOW ABOUT THE TOURNAMENT. YOUR FATHER IS SUPPOSED TO TELL YOU BUT—

IS THAT SOMEONE NEW? THERE, WITH THE TRAY?

ETHAN, PLEASE, THIS IS IMPORTANT.

NOW YOU'RE BEGINNING TO SOUND LIKE MY MOTHER, SKINK.

OPEN.

SUB-BASEMENT FORGE.

I'VE BEEN TRAINING. YOU'LL BE THERE WITH ME. I'M NOT WORRIED.

MUCH.

MAYBE YOU SHOULD BE.

WHAT'S THAT SUPPOSED TO MEAN?

SMITH? HELLO?

...BUT I SEEM TO HAVE MISPLACED MY SON.

I COULD SWEAR HE WAS A LITTLE BOY, ABOUT SO HIGH, BUT ALL I FIND IS A STRAPPING YOUNG MAN.

I WONDER IF YOU COULD TELL ME WHAT HAPPENED TO HIM.

HAPPY BIRTHDAY, ETHAN.

FATHER.

DID YOU SEE?

A BEAUTIFUL BLADE. THE SMITH'S OUTDONE HIMSELF.

I HOPE IT'S A LUCKY BLADE, TOO. ESPECIALLY IF YOU'RE STILL COMMITTED TO USING *HIM* AS YOUR SECOND.

A MEMBER OF THE LESSER RACES, ETHAN, AND COURT JESTER AT THAT. IT'S SIMPLY NOT DONE.

SKINK'S TAKEN CARE OF ME MY WHOLE LIFE.

HE'LL TAKE CARE OF ME IN THE ARENA.

YOUR YOUNGEST SON'S A MAN NOW, DANE. OLD ENOUGH TO MAKE HIS OWN DECISIONS...

...EVEN IF ONE OF THOSE DECISIONS IS TO TAKE PART IN THAT BARBARIC TOURNAMENT.

THIS AGAIN, MARIELLA?

HELLO, MOTHER. YLENA.

MAJESTY.

HAVE YOU AT LEAST TOLD HIM? MAYBE HE'LL SEE REASON.

THE TOURNAMENT'S EXISTED FOR CENTURIES. THAT YOU DON'T APPROVE OF IT DOESN'T CHANGE THE FACT THAT IT KEEPS THE PEACE BETWEEN US AND OUR NEIGHBORS TO THE EAST.

AVALON HASN'T KNOWN TRUE WARFARE SINCE RITUAL COMBAT BEGAN...

HAPPY BIRTHDAY, DEAR.

THANKS.

FROM ME AS WELL.

...AND OUR FAMILY HAS ALWAYS HAD A ROLE IN IT.

ETHAN, I'M PROUD YOU WANT TO CARRY ON OUR TRADITION, BUT YOUR MOTHER'S RIGHT. IT'S ONLY FAIR YOU KNOW WHAT AWAITS YOU.

THE TOURNAMENT DRAW MATCHES YOU AGAINST *BRON*. I DON'T HAVE TO TELL YOU HIS REPUTATION. HE *HAS* BEATEN BOTH YOUR BROTHERS IN THE PAST...

...BUT I'LL SUPPORT WHATEVER DECISION YOU MAKE. WE ALL WILL.

I'M NOT AFRAID OF BRON.

ETHAN, PAY ATTENTION. *CONCENTRATE.*

RIGHT...

...RIGHT.

COMBAT TO COMMENCE BETWEEN PRINCE ETHAN OF THE HERON DYNASTY OF THE WEST...

...AND PRINCE BRON OF THE RAVEN DYNASTY OF THE EAST.

TRADITIONAL RULES OF THE TOURNAMENT APPLY.

COMBAT IS TO FIRST BLOOD OR A YIELDING. PHYSICIANS MAY ENTER THE CIRCLE AT THEIR DISCRETION OR WHEN SUMMONED. MY DECISIONS AS ARBITER ARE FINAL AND BINDING.

IN THE NAME OF THE SURVIVORS, MAY THE PEACE BE FOREVER KEPT.

ARE THE COMBATANTS AND THEIR SECONDS PREPARED?

YES.

YES.

YOU MAY INITIATE YOUR ARMOR.

HMMMMMM

HMMMMMM

When CrossGen launched in May 2000, the goal was to debut with a splash. An initial release of four monthly titles seemed to be the right number, but asking fans to buy four comics to get a taste of a brand new universe of stories was asking a lot.

Hence, *CrossGen Chronicles* #1 offered an opportunity to sample the characters, worlds and stories surrounding *Mystic, Sigil, Scion* and *Meridian*. The issue featured five-page vignettes respectively showcasing each lead character and storyline. The trick was placing them all within the context of one story, so the choice was made to use the god-like beings of the CrossGen Universe, the First, as a framing device.

It also was decided that the five-page interludes would present the characters just after they'd been granted their sigils, allowing an exploration of how they reacted to those sigils. As far as the timeline was concerned, the sequences would fit between issues #1 and #2 of the individual series. Once the #1 issues hit the stands, perceptive readers would be able to fit together the chronology. Leaving a trail of clues for clever readers to follow would become a CrossGen hallmark.

"We used this space to portray the crowd's reaction to the result of Ethan's wounding Bron," said *Scion* writer Ron Marz. "Something like that had never happened in the history of the tournament, and that incident would be the focal point of all of the action for the next several issues, so in *Chronicles* we moved Ethan from the main hall to the catacombs inside the stadium and got our first look at the damage Ethan did to Bron's face."

Here it is, presented "in sequence" for the first time. ✐

Chapter 1.5

Chapter 2

"Ethan's tale is a coming of age story. You start off with the young prince on the cusp of manhood, on his 21st birthday suddenly thrown into a situation for which he is completely not prepared."

– *Ron Marz*

Whence Comes the Hero

If you ask *Scion* writer Ron Marz where the character of Ethan came from, he'll say, "The East."

But that's just Ron.

In truth, Ron's inspirations combine the classic and the modern as much as the look and feel of *Scion* combine elements of both fantasy and science fiction. And it's not always what you put in the stew that makes it taste good, but rather how well the ingredients taste together.

"In creating a protagonist like Ethan, we again plugged into some of those traditional Joseph Campbell concepts that are just evergreen," Ron said. "In my case, Joseph Campbell is always knocking around in the back of my head along with that Shakespeare guy. The classic stories of heroes and villains always hold a great deal of truth to them – truth with a capital T – making them universal in their appeal. Ethan's is very much the hero's journey. The family dynamics that play out in his family and the opposing Raven Dynasty are all fairly Shakespearean – sometimes intentionally so and sometimes not – because while Shakespeare was the master of practically all literary concepts, he had a particularly insightful handle on family dynamics and the dynamics of royalty. You don't read *Hamlet* without getting a sense of the intrigues and the passions that drive royal families."

But the "royal" aspect of

> "Ethan's is very much the hero's journey. The family dynamics that play out in his family and the opposing Raven Dynasty are all fairly Shakespearean – sometimes intentionally so and sometimes not – because while Shakespeare was the master of practically all literary concepts, he had a particularly insightful handle on family dynamics and the dynamics of royalty."

Scion was just part of the story's flavor. Ron was immediately drawn to *Scion* when he read the initial outline for the title. He saw the potential to make it more than simply the story of a young prince. He saw the opportunity to put a different spin on some old concepts.

"*Scion* was the book in the original CrossGen 'bible' that I immediately had the most feel for. Just reading the barest bones of the idea for the book, I could see it already," Ron said. "Ethan's tale is a coming of age story. You start off with the young prince on the cusp of manhood on his 21st birthday, suddenly thrown into a situation for which he is completely not prepared. That, to me at least, is the process of making a hero – building a character into a believable hero. I've never been one to easily embrace the 'instant hero' concept you find in superhero comics. I'm much more drawn to people who have human frailties, human foibles that must be overcome in order to make that transformation into the hero."

And, of course, when creating comic books, it's difficult not to draw some level of inspiration from the Zen master of that medium, Spider-Man co-creator Stan Lee.

"I think when you do comics, you borrow from comics, certainly, whether it's in an intentional way or a subliminal thing that creeps into what you do," Ron said. "In Ethan, we borrowed from Stan Lee's 'with great power comes great responsibility' philosophy – everyone borrows from Stan in that regard. It's such a strong vision of heroism, you can't help but borrow from that."

TREACHERY MOST BASE, THOUGH I SHOULD EXPECT NOTHING LESS FROM A SCION OF THE HERON DYNASTY.

YOUR WHELP HAS COMMITTED A GRIEVOUS BREACH OF THE TOURNAMENT'S SPIRIT, THE EVIDENCE OF IT CARVED INTO MY SON'S FACE.

DON'T THINK THIS LUDICROUS TALE OF A MYSTERIOUS MARK BRINGING POWER TEMPERS THIS SLIGHT. IF PROPER RESPONSIBILITIES AREN'T TAKEN...

...THIS AFFRONT COULD LEAD TO WIDER CONFLICT.

SPARE ME YOUR THREATS, RAVEN. MY SON GIVES HIS WORD IT WAS AN ACCIDENT!

YOU REFUSE TO EVEN ADMIT YOUR DECEIT?

WHAT HAPPENED DOES NOT MATTER!

WHAT MATTERS IS WHAT'S GOING TO BE DONE ABOUT IT!

WE DEMAND REPARATION...

...HIM, AS A PRISONER UNTIL THE NEXT TOURNAMENT IN ONE YEAR'S TIME.

ARE YOU SURE THIS IS WHAT YOU WANT TO DO? OUR DYNASTY, THE ENTIRE KINGDOM OF THE WEST, WILL STAND BEHIND YOU.

MOTHER...

...I WOULDN'T BE THE SON YOU RAISED IF I DIDN'T SHOULDER MY RESPONSIBILITIES.

I'LL BE ALL RIGHT.

YLENA?

ETHAN, JUST...

...YOU CAN'T DO THIS...

YOU KNOW OUR SISTER, ETHAN. IT'S NOT YOU SHE'S UPSET WITH.

BE STRONG.

I WILL, KAI.

ARTOR...

A MAN'S NOT MEASURED BY HIS YEARS, LITTLE BROTHER. A MAN IS MEASURED BY HIS ACTIONS.

TODAY YOU BECAME A MAN.

THIS IS THE RIGHT THING TO DO, FATHER.

GOODBYE.

I KNOW.

POLITICALLY, I KNOW. THAT DOESN'T MAKE IT ANY LESS BITTER TO SWALLOW.

YOU MAKE ME PROUD, MY SON.

IT'S OKAY, ETHAN, YOU'RE OKAY...

...EVEN YOUR FACE.

MY... FACE? WHAT DO YOU...

...IT'S HEALED.

HOW?

AND HOW DID I GET... *WHEREVER* I AM?

THERE'S WHO CAN GIVE YOU ANSWERS.

YOU'RE SAFE OUTSIDE THE KEEP.

I BROUGHT YOU HERE. I'M THE ONE WHO FREED YOU.

Chapter 3

"By issue #3, I was getting more comfortable drawing a medieval world. It's quite different from what I used to do: draw superheroes beating each other's heads in against the backdrop of New York City."

– Jim Cheung

Jim and Ron and Ethan and Bron

For *Scion* penciler Jim Cheung, submitting his initial character designs was like getting a loan approved with the first application.

"The base look of the characters had been established by Ron and the CrossGen team when they gave me the assignment to draw the first full sketches," Jim said. "Elements like Ethan's age and his long blonde hair had already been set. The details on Ethan had been sent to me in England with some notes, along with similar notes on the other characters. I did my sketches and faxed them over, and the response I got from Ron and Mark [Alessi] seemed to be very positive. We really didn't need to make any changes from there. It was quite a relief."

Jim, a veteran Marvel penciler who had recently worked on the *X-Men* spin-off title *X-Force*, faced a lot of challenges stepping up to the *Scion* plate – he had never drawn a medieval work, he had never drawn fantasy or sword and sorcery, and he had never worked in a studio.

"When the decision was made that Jim was in and he was going to be one of the first hires as a penciler, I was keen to work with him," said *Scion* writer Ron Marz. "I had seen Jim's work on *X-Force*, and I thought it was good, solid comic book

work. And then he got here, and he was so much better than the finished product at

> ## "...Jim has done such a great job of building this world and making it all believable. Everything you see in the book is his design sense, his work, and it's an exceptionally well-realized, coherent world."

Marvel ever showed. When he dug into the first issue of *Scion*, his immediate enthusiasm was evident, and he got better every issue. He's very intense, very driven, and he's his own worst critic. He's always very hard on himself. Whenever I try to give him the easy way out on a page, he won't take it. In his time here, he's easily become one of a handful of guys who could be deemed the best monthly artist working in the business today."

Part of the success of Jim's work on *Scion* also came from his front-end

research. Having no past frame of reference for drawing a medieval world, Jim hit the books.

"I looked for a lot of reference volumes and medieval-themed books and took elements from each of those to start with," Jim said. "Mark provided me a lot of reference, too. I had never drawn a medieval book before, so it was a challenge, but it's been a lot of fun. I'm still trying to get a grasp on the whole thing, constantly scouting for more reference. By issue #5 I was getting more comfortable drawing a medieval world. It's quite different from what I used to do: draw superheroes beating each other's heads in against the backdrop of New York City."

That attention to detail, and Jim's never-ending battle for a combination of authenticity and creativity, are what continues to draw people into the world of *Scion*.

"I think one of the reasons *Scion* has been so successful and has brought in a pretty loyal audience is because Jim has done such a great job of building this world and making it all believable," Ron said. "Everything you see in the book is his design sense, his work, and it's an exceptionally well-realized, coherent world."

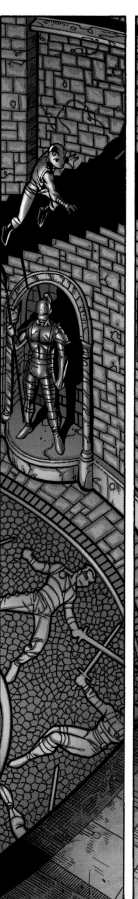

WHAT *IS* THIS PLACE?

HELL.

THIS IS HOW THE LESSER RACES ARE WORKED IN THE EAST. HERE THEY'RE MINING ORE...

"...TRAPPED IN SUNLESS CAVERNS, GUARDS READY TO PUT THE LASH TO THEIR BACKS."

"BUT THEY COULD JUST AS EASILY BE TOILING IN FIELDS, OR IN FACTORIES. WHAT YOU'RE LOOKING AT ISN'T UNUSUAL...

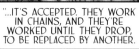

"...IT'S ACCEPTED. THEY WORK IN CHAINS, AND THEY'RE WORKED UNTIL THEY DROP, TO BE REPLACED BY ANOTHER."

"ISN'T OUR SCIENCE GLORIOUS?

"IT'S ALLOWED US TO MAKE *DISPOSABLE LIFE.*"

THE LESSER RACES WERE GENETICALLY ENGINEERED SO WE WOULDN'T HAVE TO GET OUR HANDS DIRTY.

"WE BRED THEM TO BE JUST WHAT WE NEEDED, TO BE A *NEW* KIND OF PERSON...

"...AND NOW WE CONSIDER THEM LESS THAN HUMAN."

...IF WE DIDN'T RUN INTO BRON.

THEY'VE GOT US TRAPPED, SKINK.

YOU'VE HEALED YOUR SCAR, I SEE. I DIDN'T *HAVE* THE SAME OPTION.

YOU SHOULD HAVE KEPT YOUR PLACE, BOY.

YOUR ESCAPE IS SETTING MY KINGDOM AND YOURS ON THE ROAD TO WAR.

EASY, BOY.

BUT...

...WHY ISN'T IT...?

ASHLEIGH?

YES, I KNOW, I'M GLAD TO SEE YOU, TOO.

YOU RUN ALONG NOW, OKAY?

HOW DID YOU DO THAT?

ANIMALS *LIKE* ME.

Chapter 4

"After drawing regular-sized people all the time, getting a chance to draw this giant character with ridiculous proportions is a nice break."

– Jim Cheung

Enter the Anti-Hero

There's just something about a good anti-hero.

Maybe it's because you can never tell whether he's a good guy, a bad guy, or something in between. Perhaps it's the edginess, the unpredictability of the character. Sometimes it's just the appearance of the character that's particularly striking.

Exeter, the bounty hunter introduced in *Scion* #4, has all those qualities and more. And for *Scion* writer Ron Marz and penciler Jim Cheung, he's just a boatload of fun to write and draw.

"I cribbed the name Exeter from *Henry V*, one of my favorite Shakespeare plays," Ron said. "He was really intended to be a one-off character," Ron said. "He was going to be someone who showed up to be an antagonist for Ethan and then go away, but he came off so well it seemed foolish to discard the character, so we brought him back again. He'll have a much greater role in the future of the book than anyone expected."

The look of Exeter was one part Ron and one part Jim; the character's face came from a composite of some of the early unused character sketches actually done to develop Ethan's companion, Skink.

"The design of Exeter's face was originally one of the

> **"[Exeter] was going to be someone who showed up to be an antagonist for Ethan and then go away, but he came off so well it seemed foolish to discard the character, so we brought him back again. He'll have a much greater role in the future of the book than anyone expected."**

choices for Skink's face," Ron recalled. "Jim came up with a bunch of different head shots for what our humpbacked little sidekick was going to look like. It wasn't right for Skink, but we said, 'We're using that. We don't know where – we'll find a place.' So we just made him eight feet tall."

The rest of Exeter, his massive bulk, came from Ron's love of those types of big, bulky villains from comic books past.

"It came from, I think, one of my favorite character types – that big, thick, almost impossibly bulky villain, what I think of as the Jim Starlin type – Marvel's Thanos or Jack Kirby's Darkseid in DC *The New Gods*. That was the body type I was looking for."

For Jim, drawing Exeter was like having a nice chocolate chip cookie. After laboring away all day on costumes that rely on technical detail and exact proportionate scale, Jim was able to throw all the rules out the window with Exeter. His body type followed no real-world logic, so Jim had the opportunity to go to town on him.

"Ron asked for an eight-foot character, and some bad guys always have this extra thing, this mysterious attitude – it was just something that felt right," Jim said. "It's pretty fun doing a big, hulking character. After drawing regular-sized people all the time, getting a chance to draw this giant character with ridiculous proportions is a nice break. I mean, his hands tend to be bigger than his head! Between the fun that Ron has writing him and the fun I have drawing him, I think we can count on Exeter being around for a long time."

LAST TIME I *EVER*...

PWUH!

AH!

...GO, SKINK!...

BRON'S ANXIOUS TO SEE YOU AGAIN, HERON.

THOUGH I DOUBT YOUR *NEXT* STAY IN RAVEN KEEP WILL BE AS PLEASANT.

OR AS BRIEF.

...BED DOWN FOR THE NIGHT...

ARRR!

...IN AN ABANDONED CASTLE!

95

THAT WAS *MY* FAULT. EVERYONE ON THIS SIDE OF THE GREAT OCEAN IS LOOKING FOR US...

...AND MY FIRST REACTION WAS TO ASSUME THE BOUNTY HUNTER WAS WITH THE UNDERGROUND JUST BECAUSE HE WAS OF THE LESSER RACES.

I HAVE TO BE A LOT MORE CAREFUL IF I'M GOING TO GET US HOME.

IT'S A MISTAKE ANYONE COULD HAVE MADE, ETHAN.

IT'S A MISTAKE ANYONE WHO'S THINKING TOO MUCH ABOUT THE UNDERGROUND COULD HAVE MADE.

AFTER WHAT I SAW...AFTER WHAT ASHLEIGH SHOWED ME IN THE MINES...

ASHLEIGH ASKED FOR MY HELP BECAUSE THE LESSER RACES ARE SLAVES IN THE EAST.

AND I TURNED HER DOWN.

YOU UNDERSTAND WHY I DID THAT, RIGHT, SKINK?

I UNDERSTAND YOU HAVE A GREAT DEAL OF RESPONSIBILITY ON YOUR SHOULDERS.

I'VE TOLD YOU THIS BEFORE, ETHAN. YOU DIDN'T *ASK* FOR WHAT HAPPENED TO YOU. I'M SORRY ABOUT THAT.

IN MANY WAYS THE PATH YOU FOLLOW HAS BEEN TAKEN OUT OF YOUR HANDS. YOUR DESTINY'S NOT YOUR OWN ANYMORE.

YOU'RE TALKING ABOUT THE MARK I HAVE?

I KNOW IT GRANTS *POWER* SOME- HOW... IT EVEN HEALED MY FACE WHEN BRON CUT ME.

IT'S CHANGED MY LIFE...

...BUT I STILL DON'T UNDERSTAND WHAT IT REALLY IS.

I THINK IT CAN BE WHAT YOU MAKE OF IT. A GIFT *OR* A CURSE.

WELL, EITHER WAY, I HOPE IT MIGHT MAKE A DIFFERENCE IN THIS WAR THE RAVENS WANT TO START.

THOUGH IF WE CAN GET TO A BOAT AND MAKE OUR WAY HOME, MAYBE WAR CAN *STILL* BE AVERTED.

YOU THINK THAT'S THE RIGHT THING TO DO, SKINK? GOING HOME?

ETHAN...

WE SHOULD BE ABLE TO REACH THE VILLAGE DOWN THERE BEFORE THE SUN'S FULLY UP AND THIS FOG BURNS OFF.

THEN WE JUST FIND A HOVERSHIP AND SLIP AWAY WITH IT. I'M PRETTY SURE I CAN PILOT ONE WELL ENOUGH TO CROSS THE GREAT SEA AND GET US...

...oh.

Oh, no...

THERE'S AN ENTIRE ARMY DOWN THERE, ETHAN. ARE YOU SURE WALKING RIGHT INTO THE MIDST OF IT IS THE WISEST PLAN?

WHAT ELSE DO YOU EXPECT ME TO DO?

HO! STAND AND BE RECOGNIZED! WHO APPROACHES?

NO ONE, SIRE...

...ONLY A SERVANT BEARING A MESSAGE FROM BRON.

BRON *HIMSELF?* WHY WOULD HE SEND A SLAVE TO DELIVER—

CHN!

CHONK

I'M FAIRLY CERTAIN NO ONE ELSE HEARD, BUT LET'S BE QUICK ABOUT THIS ALL THE SAME.

ANY OF THE SHIPS HERE WILL SERVE.

YOU THERE!

WHO ARE YOU? WHAT'S YOUR BUSINESS WITH THE SCOUT-SHIP?

STEALING IT.

PWHH!

WHAT'S *YOUR* BUSINESS WITH THE SCOUT-SHIP?

SKINK! THESE ARE THE INVASION PLANS! EVEN THE LANDING SITE!

GET IN, I'LL SHUT DOWN THE MAGNETIC MOORING SO WE CAN CAST OFF AND BE—

SHUNKK

KRAKOOSH

SPLOOSH

IT COULDN'T TAKE HIS WEIGHT! I THINK MAYBE HE'S—

I'VE *NEVER* LOST A BOUNTY!

HRRR!

MY *FAMILY* NEEDS ME...

"...WE'RE GOING HOME."

Chapter 5

"The ironic thing was that this issue actually represented for me the calm *before* the storm – issue #6 was slated to be the big battle issue, and aside from killing some combatants I was sure that issue #6 was going to kill me."

– *Jim Cheung*

The Imperfect Storm

Before moving on to Chapter 5, perhaps now would be a good time for a restroom break. If you don't need it now, you will soon.

One of the centerpieces in the *Scion* series thus far has been a sequence from issue #5 involving Ethan, Skink, and a massive storm at sea. Many fans have theorized that *Scion* writer Ron Marz and penciler Jim Cheung were inspired to do the sequence after seeing the George Clooney film *The Perfect Storm*. Well, they were half right.

"I think part of the inspiration for that sequence was the movie poster for *The Perfect Storm*, with that great shot of the boat going up that massive wave," Ron said. "A lot of people thought we imitated the movie for that sequence, but at that time, none of us had seen it. That issue of *Scion* was in the can before the movie came out. It was actually about a year later when I eventually saw the movie on cable, and frankly I think we did a better job than they did."

Drawing an entire issue in which Ethan and Skink are being tossed around by Mother Nature wasn't exactly an easy chore for the art team, either. It came with certain, um, hazards.

"I did enjoy drawing that sequence because it just seemed fun doing

something different," Jim said. "The challenge was to keep a steady flow with the

> "What we were trying to do with that book was develop a new way of portraying rain – overlapping one sequence of rain over the other – and it's established a great new realistic way of showing rainfall in a comic book."

storm throwing things about, but it was definitely a very fun issue. The ironic thing was that this issue actually represented for me the calm *before* the storm – issue #6 was slated to be the big battle issue, and aside from killing some combatants I was sure that issue #6 was going to kill me."

Perhaps issue #5 was hardest on *Scion* colorist Caesar Rodriguez.

"Jimmy was working on that particular 'Big Wave' double-page spread for about a week," recalled

Caesar. "What we were trying to do with that book was develop a new way of portraying rain – overlapping one sequence of rain over the other – an it's established a great new realistic way of showing rainfall in a comic book. It also something I'm seeing other studios that work on competitors' comic books picking up now. I also saw being done on Bart Sears' book (CrossGen's *The First*), which is kind of coo because it means that we actually started a new way of doing things. To look a it that way, it's kind of fun That storm was quite a challenge – it was difficult to keep the water looking like water. We also wanted to look violent and dark so that everybody else gets th feeling that this storm is ar ominous-looking thing."

And then there were th constant interruptions.

"Of course, when I looked at water all the time, working on all those pages, I had to go to the restroom every half-hour for the better part of the month," Caesar said. "I kept looking at it and my body kept responding. I had the same feeling when I went to see *Titanic* the first time. That was a three-hour movie! You don't dare drink that 72-ounce 7-Up they give you at the theater. The second time I went, I said, 'No B Gulp for me!'"

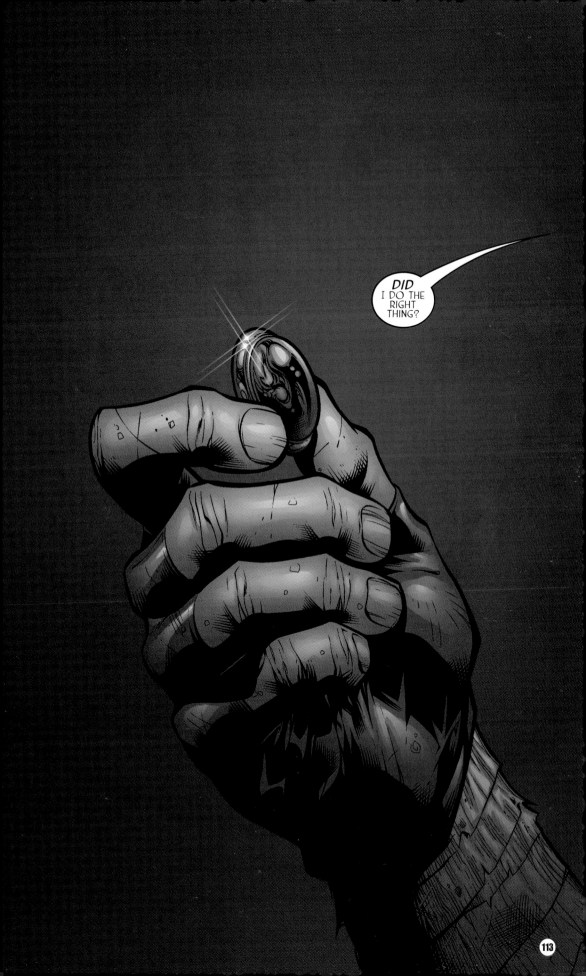

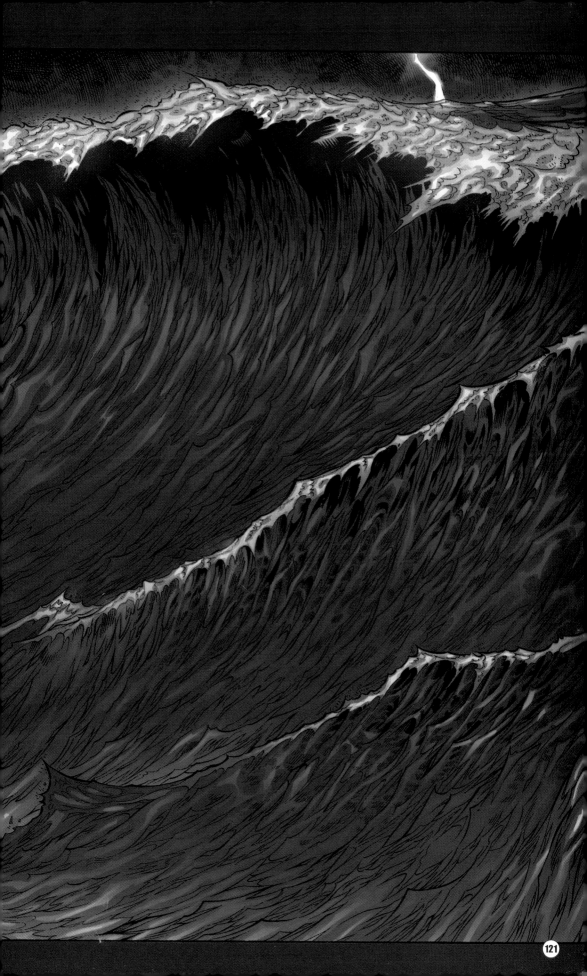

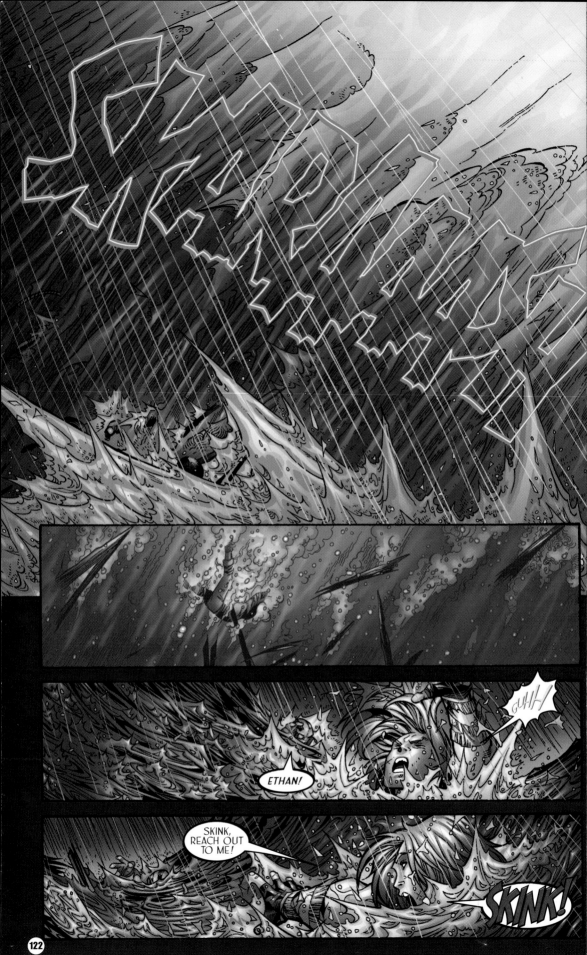

ETHAN?

ETHAN.

ARE YOU ALL RIGHT?

I'M...

...NNF...

...I'M OKAY. I THINK.

SKINK, I REMEMBER THE SHIP BEING SWAMPED, AND THEN SINKING. THERE WERE *PEOPLE* UNDERWATER.

THEY SAVED ME, STUCK ME WITH SOMETHING THAT LET ME BREATHE, AND I THINK MAYBE IT PUT ME TO SLEEP TOO. BUT NOT BEFORE I SAW A *CITY* DOWN THERE.

IS THAT POSSIBLE? COULD AN UNDERSEA LESSER RACE HAVE BUILT A SECRET CITY?

GOOD BOY, HOGARTH.

FATHER DOESN'T RIDE YOU AS MUCH AS HE—

YLENA!

STRANGE.

I KNOW IT MUST BE THE WIND COMING OFF THE SEA, BUT THAT SOUNDS JUST LIKE...

...MY BROTHER.

YLENA! HERE!

ETHAN.

ETHAN, WHAT *HAPPENED?!* WHERE'VE YOU *BEEN?!*

EASY. ONE AT A TIME, OKAY?

IT'S JUST... oh, ETHAN I'M SO GLAD TO SEE YOU.

WE WERE ALL SO WORRIED. THE RAVENS SAID YOU ESCAPED, WE THOUGHT YOU MIGHT EVEN BE DEAD.

ALMOST. NOT QUITE.

HOW'S EVERYONE ELSE?

THE FAMILY'S WELL... EXCEPT FOR BEING CONCERNED FOR YOU, OF COURSE.

BUT YOU SHOULD KNOW THE SITUATION ISN'T GOOD. BECAUSE OF EVERYTHING THAT'S HAPPENED...

...FATHER'S GATHERED EVERYONE IN THE WAR CHAMBERS.

MOTHER! FATHER!

SORRY FOR THE INTERRUPTION...

...BUT I THOUGHT YOU'D WANT TO SEE WHO WASHED UP ON THE BEACH.

THE BEACH? WHAT ARE YOU...

...TALKING ABOUT?

HAH! WHAT KIND OF BAIT HAULS IN A CATCH LIKE *THAT*, SISTER?

IT *CAN'T* BE...

ETHAN! THANK THE ANCESTORS YOU'RE ALIVE.

SKINK MADE SURE I *STAYED* THAT WAY, MOTHER.

I PROMISED HE WOULD BE SAFE. I KEPT MY WORD.

WE'RE INDEBTED TO YOU, SKINK.

FATHER, YOU DON'T UNDERSTAND. THEY'RE ALREADY ON THEIR WAY.

WHAT?

AND I KNOW WHERE THEY MEAN TO LAND THEIR INVASION FORCE.

ETHAN, WHAT CAN YOU REALLY *DO?* THEY'RE SAYING YOU ESCAPED, AND HERE YOU ARE. THE *TRUTH* ISN'T GOING TO MATTER.

THE RAVENS HAVE BEEN SPOILING FOR A FIGHT FOR DECADES. THEY'VE JUST NEVER HAD A CONVENIENT EXCUSE UNTIL NOW.

WE'VE BEEN HERE TRYING TO PREPARE, IF IT COMES TO THAT.

THE HOVERSHIP I STOLE WAS THE ADVANCE SCOUTSHIP FOR THE RAVEN FLEET. I GOT MY HANDS ON DOCUMENTS NAMING THE LANDING SITE.

THEY'RE GOING TO MARSHAL *HERE...*

...AT POINT KORDAY.

YOU'VE DONE WELL, MY SON. YOU'VE GIVEN US THE ADVANTAGE OF SURPRISE.

BUT ISN'T THERE STILL SOME WAY TO AVOID ALL THIS?

Chapter 6

"It's easy for me to write two-page battle sequences, but the hard work they put into it resulted in one of the most incredible-looking books I've ever seen."

– *Ron Marz*

War is Hell

If *Scion* artist Jim Cheung had really given it some thought, he might have wondered if writer Ron Marz had some kind of grudge against him.

Ron had written a storyline for the previous five issues of *Scion* that was going to culminate in issue #6 with a war between the Raven Dynasty and the Heron Dynasty. Ethan vs. Bron, army against army, for all the marbles.

So Ron brainstormed a story that would result in the creation of one of the most astounding artistic triumphs in CrossGen's short history. Easy for him. He didn't have to draw it.

"I came up with the idea of doing the entire issue as the battle that takes place," Ron said. "Originally, I wanted the whole story to be silent, but trying to convey the emotion of the issue as well as the spectacle made it a little awkward. Then I thought of doing the whole issue as double-page spreads – not only because Jim is so good at arranging spreads but because I wanted to portray as much as possible that widescreen spectacle you got in *Braveheart* or *Gladiator* or *Spartacus*. And feeling that it's not fair to inflict that on Jim without his consent, I asked him first. He nodded and said what he always says: ''salright.'

Obviously the burden of the real work on the issue fell on the art team and

---

"Oh, sure, it was a great comic book, and when I saw those pages come in from Jimmy, I thought, 'Wow, this is some of the most beautiful comic book work I've ever seen' – but my second thought was, 'I have to ink this. I'm going to die.'"

---

substantially on Jim. It's easy for me to write two-page battle sequences, but the hard work they put into it resulted in one of the most incredible-looking books I've ever seen."

When asked why Jim agreed to do the issue completely as two-page spreads – an exercise that had Jim working through the night every night for the better part of a month and a half – he's still not quite sure why he said yes.

"It was certainly a challenge," Jim said, "that's

for sure. Executing the issue was just a case of trying to cram in as much detail as possible because of the magnitude of the story."

Among the details included were computer terminals on the flying dragons, referenced armaments specific to the Raven and Heron armies, and a variety of weaponry taken right out of history and then mixed with Jim's own sensibilities.

"Those computers on the dragons were almost forgotten, but they were just little things that were easy to fix," Jim said. "Ultimately, there were some things I would have changed. If I were to do i again, I'd want to do it in tabloid-sized book to get more detail into the whole battle. I just like the opportunity to do my bes work and make it look as good as I can."

Scion inker Don Hillsman II, however, thought there was another plan at work.

"Jim's trying to kill us,' Don said. "There was no other explanation. Oh, sure, it was a great comic book, and when I saw those pages come in from Jimmy, I thought, 'Wow, this is some of the most beautiful comic book wor I've ever seen' – but my second thought was, 'I have to ink this. I'm going to die.'" ☽

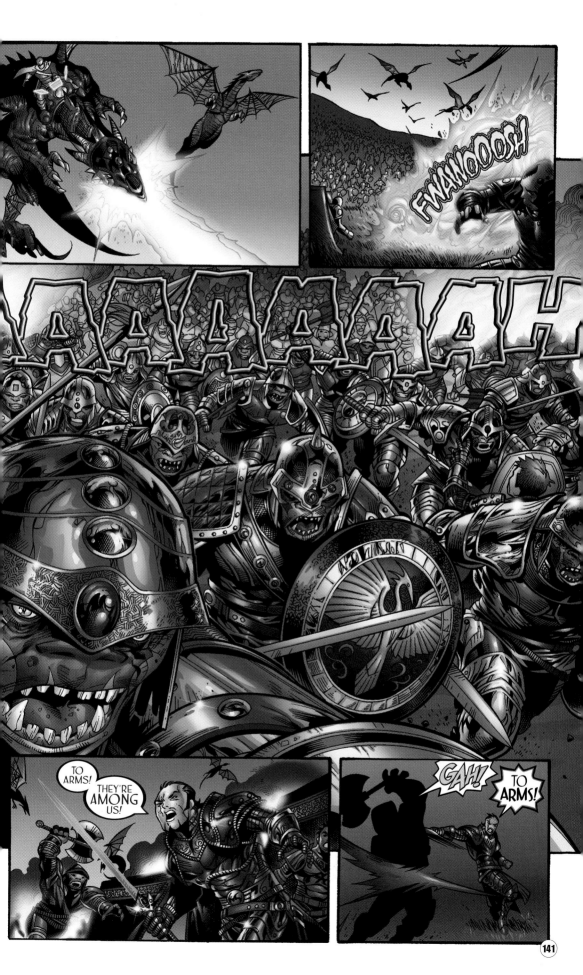

THE SHOCK TROOPS AND DRAGONS SHOULD THROW THE ENTIRE ENCAMPMENT INTO CHAOS.

WHEN WE SWEEP IN WE'LL TURN IT INTO A *ROUT*.

THAT *BRAND* ON YOUR ARM, ETHAN, WILL IT HELP US IN THIS BATTLE?

I'M STILL NOT EXACTLY SURE *WHAT* IT CAN DO.

...THE TROOPS WILL LOOK TO *US*. THE BATTLE OF POINT KORDAY WILL BE A GLORIOUS MARK IN HERON HISTORY IF WE *LEAD BY DEED*.

I'M READY.

EYAA!

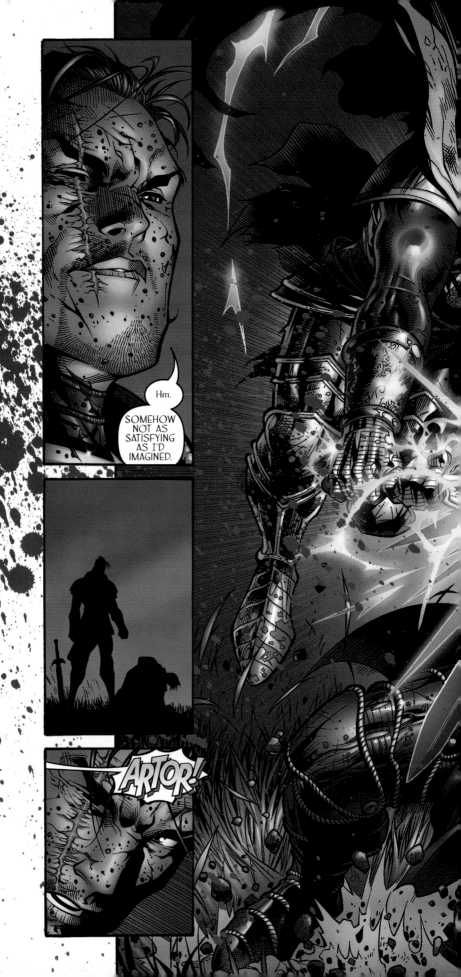

Hm. SOMEHOW NOT AS SATISFYING AS I'D IMAGINED.

ARTOR!

Chapter 7

Among the traditional comic book ideas trounced by CrossGen Comics through *Scion* was the notion of death.

In many comics, characters die only to be brought back on a whim. After all, it's a comic book, so the rules of the real world don't apply, right? Well, not anymore. If comic books are going to show violence, they should also show the consequences of that violence, according to writer Ron Marz.

"The funeral issue was obviously the flip side to the battle issue – very much the aftermath and more character-driven than action-driven," Ron said. "I drew upon funerals I've been to where I've said goodbye to loved ones, specifically that of my father – the closest person to me who's ever passed away. I tried to put that emotional content into the book as much as possible. Having a son myself, I can't imagine what it must be like to bury your son. I can't think of anything more horrific. That's essentially what we wanted to portray in this issue – the emotional fallout from that kind of loss. We didn't just want to pass off this death as yet another comic-book death where the corpse gets trotted out a few years later, having undergone a miraculous revival. We wanted this death to be as real as possible in comic-book terms." ●

SLAIN IN
BATTLE

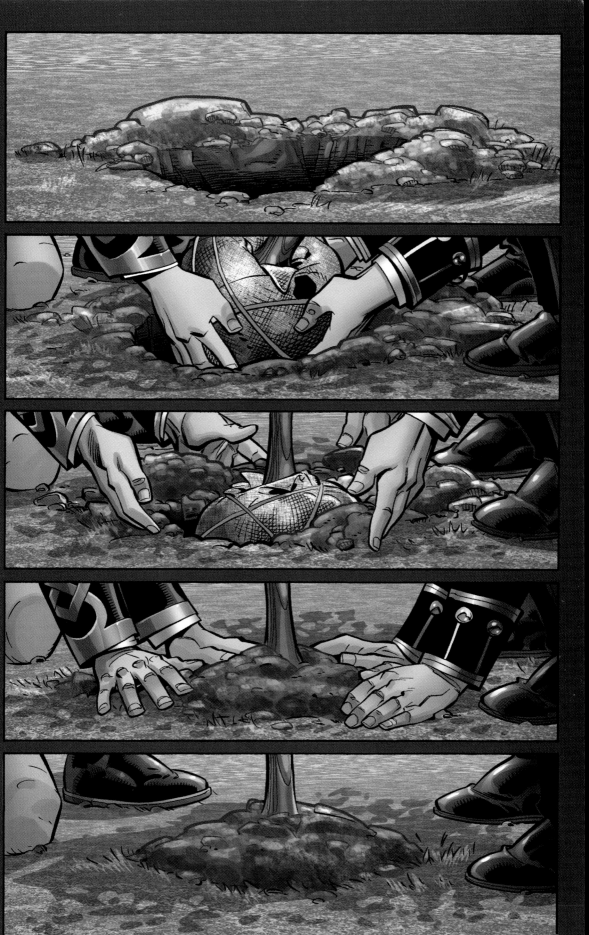

ARTOR WAS ALWAYS FOND OF THIS GROVE. I THINK HE LIKED THE SENSE OF HISTORY HERE...

...A TREE IN REMEMBRANCE OF EACH FALLEN MEMBER OF OUR DYNASTY. SOME OF THESE ARE HUNDREDS OF YEARS OLD.

I CAN'T IMAGINE HE SAW *HIMSELF* BEING REMEMBERED HERE, KAI. OR THAT I'D BE THE CAUSE OF IT.

NONE OF THIS WOULD'VE HAPPENED...

...WE WOULDN'T BE BURYING OUR BROTHER...

...IF NOT FOR ME.

THERE'S NO USE IN WORRYING YOURSELF OVER "*IF*," ETHAN.

YOU WERE THE FLASHPOINT, NOT THE CAUSE. TENSIONS BETWEEN THE KINGDOMS WERE BREWING LONG BEFORE YOUR INVOLVEMENT.

IF *YOU* HADN'T SERVED TO SET IT OFF, SOMETHING ELSE WOULD HAVE.

BUT IT'S ALL JUST SO...I DON'T KNOW.

POINTLESS.

WHAT DID WE ACCOMPLISH AT POINT KORDAY? WE WON A BATTLE, BUT THE WAR'S GOING TO GO ON.

THIS TIME IT WAS ARTOR. NEXT TIME, SOMEONE ELSE. HOW MANY MORE PEOPLE NEED TO DIE?

AND I CAN'T HELP THINKING ABOUT THE GIRL I MET, ASHLEIGH. AND ABOUT THE SLAVERY OF THE LESSER RACES IN THE EAST.

THERE'S SO MUCH I NEED TO THINK ABOUT.

I THINK YOU THINK *TOO MUCH*, LITTLE BROTHER.

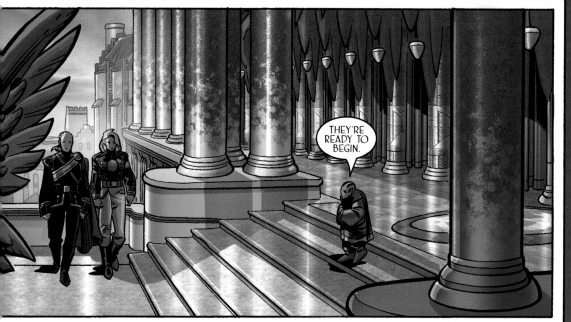

THEY'RE READY TO BEGIN.

HOW ARE OUR PARENTS HOLDING UP, SKINK?

YOUR FATHER DOES HIS BEST TO MAINTAIN A STOIC FAÇADE. HE UNDERSTANDS THAT RIGHT NOW HE MUST BE A KING FIRST AND A FATHER SECOND.

AND YOUR MOTHER...

...YOUR MOTHER IS AS YOU WOULD EXPECT.

WHAT ABOUT YOU, ETHAN? HOW ARE *YOU* HOLDING UP?

AS WELL AS I CAN, SKINK...

...CONSIDERING I HOLD MYSELF TO BLAME.

FATHER...

...IT'S DONE.

THANK YOU, MY SON. BOTH OF YOU.

I KNOW YOUR BROTHER WOULD APPRECIATE IT.

WE'LL GET THROUGH TH MOTHER.

BE STRONG, YLENA...

...WE ALL HAVE TO BE STRONG NOW.

I KNOW, ETHAN. I KNOW WE WILL.

THIS *WILL* MAKE YOU STRONGER, ETHAN.

I REALIZE I AM A LUCKY MAN. I AM BLESSED WITH THREE OTHER CHILDREN, WHO PROVIDE ME WITH SOLACE.

AND YET WHAT CONSOLATION I DERIVE FROM THEM IS TEMPERED BY THEIR OWN PAIN, FOR THEY HAVE LOST A BELOVED SIBLING.

"ALL MY CHILDREN FOUGHT VALIANTLY IN THE VICTORY SO BITTERLY WON AT POINT KORDAY. BUT RATHER THAN CELEBRATING TRIUMPH, MY DAUGHTER GRIEVES...

"...AS DO MY SONS.

"ONE CAN TAKE NO PLEASURE IN BEING A HERO OF THAT VICTORY...

"...AND THE OTHER MUST NOW BEAR THE BURDEN OF BEING HEIR TO THE THRONE."

MOST OFTEN TRAGEDY HAS NO SIRE. MOST OFTEN WE'RE LEFT TO QUESTION WHY ONE SO NOBLE LIES IN HIS COFFIN, WHY A FAMILY AND A KINGDOM SHOULD SUFFER SO.

BUT NOT THIS TIME. THIS TIME WE KNOW THE CAUSE OF OUR PAIN. WE KNOW OUR FOE'S ABJECT BRUTALITY...

"...SO CRUEL THAT A LOVING MOTHER STILL WEEPS AT THE SAVAGERY OF HER ELDEST CHILD'S DEMISE.

"Oh YES, WE KNOW OUR ENEMY OF OLD. WE HAVE MET AND DEFEATED HIM IN THIS FIRST CLASH...

"...BUT THE WAR IS NOT YET WON. WE MUST REMAIN STEADFAST, FOR THE RAVENS POSSESS MALICE AND GUILE IN EQUAL MEASURE."

LET THIS, THEN, BE OUR STRENGTH.

LET ARTOR'S DEATH BE THE BANNER WE CARRY FORWARD INTO THIS CONFLICT. WHEN WE ARE PRESSED, LET US DRAW COURAGE FROM THE SACRIFICE ALREADY MADE.

TODAY WE BURY OUR DEAD...

I'M THE ONE TO EXACT VENGEANCE, FATHER.

I'LL GO FIND BRON AND REPAY HIM IN KIND. BLOOD FOR BLOOD.

ETHAN, WE ALL RESPECT YOUR DESIRE TO PUNISH YOUR BROTHER'S KILLER. THE SAME FIRE BURNS IN MY BELLY.

BUT I CAN'T ALLOW IT. YOU LEFT OUR LANDS ONCE, AND WE'RE LUCKY YOU RETURNED TO US ALIVE.

I WON'T LET YOU LEAVE HOME AGAIN.

BUT I'M AT THE *HEART* OF EVERYTHING.

ARTOR NEVER WOULD HAVE DIED IF *I* HADN'T SET ALL THIS INTO MOTION.

IT'S *MY* RESPONSIBILITY TO AVENGE IT.

I'M THE OLDEST NOW, ETHAN. THAT DUTY SHOULD FALL TO ME.

YOU CAN'T DO THIS *BECAUSE* YOU'RE THE OLDEST, KAI.

YOU'RE NEXT IN LINE OF SUCCESSION.

ETHAN, LISTEN TO ME. I BROUGHT ARTOR INTO THIS WORLD. THE BABY I SUCKLED AT MY BREAST BLED HIS LIFE OUT ONTO THE MUD.

I KNOW YOUR HEART IS SCARRED, BUT THERE IS NO GREATER HEARTACHE THAN THAT OF A PARENT BURYING A CHILD.

I WANT ARTOR AVENGED AS MUCH AS ANY OF YOU DO. BUT NOT AT THE EXPENSE OF *EITHER* OF MY REMAINING SONS, *OR* MY DAUGHTER.

IN ALL TRUTH, ETHAN...

...YOU *ARE* FAR TOO VALUABLE TO RISK ON SOME VENDETTA.

WHO?

WHO ARE YOU?! HOW DID YOU GET IN HERE?!

ANSWER ME. OR MY BROTHER ISN'T THE ONLY ONE WHO'LL BE LAID TO REST THIS DAY.

MY APOLOGIES.

I HAD NO WISH TO INTRUDE ON YOUR PRIVACY AT SUCH A PAINFUL TIME. BUT IT'S QUITE IMPORTANT I SPEAK WITH YOUR FAMILY.

RELEASE HIM, KAI.

AT LEAST GIVE HIM THE OPPORTUNITY TO EXPLAIN HIMSELF.

THOUGH I WARN YOU, I HAD BEST FIND THE EXPLANATION A SATISFACTORY ONE.

OF COURSE. AGAIN...

...MY APOLOGIES.

MY NAME IS BERND RECHTS.

DO I KNOW YOU, SIRE?

I DON'T THINK SO.

I THINK PERHAPS I *DO.*

YOU MUST BE MISTAKEN. I'M A STRANGER HERE.

I'VE COME FROM AFAR...

...TO OFFER YOU MY AID.

I'VE NO LOVE LOST FOR THE OPPONENT IN THIS STRUGGLE. SO I MAKE MYSELF AVAILABLE TO YOU AS A COUNSELOR OF WAR.

YOU WISH TO *HELP* US AGAINST THE RAVENS.

AGAINST THE RAVENS, YES.

WHY DO WE NEED *YOU?*

BECAUSE YOU'VE NOT MADE WAR IN YOUR LIFETIMES. BECAUSE YOU WON THE VICTORY ONLY WITH SURPRISE AS YOUR ALLY...

...AND BECAUSE THE GIFT HE BEARS COULD BE A PIVOTAL ADVANTAGE IF PROPERLY HARNESSED.

AS I SAID, ETHAN, YOU'RE FAR TOO VALUABLE. YOUR PLACE MUST BE HERE.

YOU MEAN BECAUSE OF THIS? THIS THING STARTED THE CHAIN OF EVENTS THAT LED US TO THIS TOMB.

I'M BEGINNING TO THINK IT'S MORE A CURSE THAN A GIFT. AND FRANKLY, I'M NO CLOSER TO UNDERSTANDING WHAT IT TRULY IS, OR WHAT IT CAN DO.

THE SIGIL COULD BE A VERY POTENT WEAPON IN THIS WAR.

IT COULD MEAN VICTORY TO ONE SIDE OR THE OTHER.

FORGIVE ME, SIR, BUT I DON'T FIND THESE MATTERS TO BE ANY OF YOUR CONCERN.

Oh, I THINK YOU'LL FIND THAT THEY ARE—

THIS CHANGES NOTHING. I STILL INTEND TO HAVE BRON'S LIFE FOR ARTOR'S DEATH.

ETHAN...

...YOUR MOTHER AND I HAVE BURIED ONE SON. WE'RE NOT ANXIOUS TO BURY ANOTHER.

YOU DID BURY A SON. I BURIED A BROTHER.

AND IT CAN'T GO UNPUNISHED.

THAT'S WHAT YOU SAID, ISN'T IT? THAT'S WHAT YOU TOLD THE PEOPLE, FATHER. TODAY WE MOURN, TOMORROW WE TURN OUR THOUGHTS TO VENGEANCE.

YOU WANT THE PEOPLE TO RALLY TO THE CAUSE. I'M NOT ONLY YOUR SON, I'M ALSO A SUBJECT OF THIS REALM.

WHY STOP ME FROM DOING EXACTLY WHAT YOU'VE ASKED?

YOU PUT ME IN THE POSITION OF CHOOSING BETWEEN BEING A MONARCH AND BEING A FATHER.

WHAT I TELL THE PEOPLE, I TELL THEM FOR THE GOOD OF OUR KINGDOM. WE'VE NOT KNOWN WAR FOR GENERATIONS, ETHAN. THE PEOPLE ARE UNPREPARED FOR THE COST THAT ACCOMPANIES IT.

AS DISTASTEFUL AS IT MIGHT BE, I'VE USED ARTOR'S DEATH TO MUSTER THEIR SUPPORT. SLAYING BRON WOULD SERVE TO INTENSIFY IT.

HERE...

...I IMAGINE YOU'LL NEED THIS.

I IMAGINE...

...SINCE I'M GOING TO KILL A MAN WITH IT.

I'M SURE YOU DON'T NEED TO HEAR THIS, BUT I NEED TO SAY IT. WHEN YOU FIND BRON, DON'T TAKE HIM LIGHTLY *DESPITE* WHATEVER POWER THAT THING ON YOUR ARM GIVES YOU.

HATE MAKES YOU RECKLESS.

I'LL REMEMBER.

KAI, IF THE FAMILY REALLY NEEDS ME... YOU KNOW I'LL COME BACK.

OF COURSE I KNOW THAT.

TAKE CARE OF EVERYONE WHILE I'M GONE.

I WILL. YOU TAKE CARE OF *YOURSELF* WHILE YOU'RE GONE, LITTLE BROTHER.

LOOK AFTER HIM, SKINK.

I ALWAYS HAVE.

WE'VE NO TIME TO DALLY, ETHAN. MUCH AWAITS US IN THE EAST.

YOU GO AHEAD. I'LL...

...CATCH UP.

Armor-covered Covers

Making comic books is fun. Selling them is hard, which is why the cover is one of its single most important elements. For a new comic book from a new company with no track record and high expectations, the cover needs to do everything but sing and dance.

Scion's covers had elements of two different genres to convey as well as a sense of spectacle and scope. In *Scion*, sword and sorcery, one of comic-dom's tried-and-true genres, collided headlong with science fiction, creating an unusual world where technology and medievalism co-existed.

"You have to give the reader an idea of what is inside the issue without giving away main story points inappropriately," said CrossGen art director Brandon Peterson. "We sometimes don't use the cover image on the inside of the book exactly as it's portrayed, but it always gives the gist of what's inside."

One of the most outstanding covers in the initial seven issues of *Scion* was that of issue #6. Because of the comic book direct market solicitation process, the vast majority of comic book covers are drawn sometimes as early as three months before the actual issue is drawn. The cover has to be available for Diamond Distribution to include in its monthly

---

"[The cover to issue #6] has probably helped us sell thousands more comic books all around the world. The work that Jim, Don and Caesar did on that cover captured a majesty and a heroism so strong that it has become a symbol of what CrossGen Comics are all about: telling stories of true heroism and the use of power for the good of us all."

---

catalog, and the catalog is printed months in advance of the actual comic book's release.

So when *Scion* penciler Jim Cheung drew that cover, he knew the issue would be composed of double-page spreads and that a lot of hard work would be going into the issue. However, the issue hadn't been started yet, so Jim decided the cover would have to be worthy of the work that was to come. *Scion* inker Don Hillsman II and colorist Caesar Rodriguez equally stepped up their efforts and produced a singular image that is one of the most powerful produced by CrossGen Comics.

"It was simply a case of being given a description of the issue and coming up with a striking enough image," Jim said. "It was actually just a bit of luck because it all seemed to come together after that. It was something I couldn't really rush because I was trying to get across a Frank Frazetta feel with the composition if not the execution."

And if the point of the cover is to sell comic books, then *Scion* #6 has succeeded far beyond expectations.

"Not only have we sold out of that particular issue, but we've also used that image as a retail display poster to promote our entire line of comics," said CrossGen vice president Tony Panaccio. "That image has probably helped us sell thousands more comic books all around the world. The work that Jim, Don and Caesar did on that cover captured a majesty and a heroism so strong that it has become a symbol of what CrossGen Comics are all about: telling stories of true heroism and the use of power for the good of us all."

SLAIN IN
BATTLE

EXETER
Pin-up by Associate Penciler
Andrea Di Vito.
Inked by Don Hillsman II
and colored by
Caesar Rodriguez.